Mama's Shawl

By Idil Ismail
Illustrated by Wenny Stefanie

MOSAIC
PUBLISHERS

This book is dedicated to my mother, Qaali. Her name is fitting of what she is to me.

What is a Garbasaar?
A garbasaar is a large rectangular shawl that Somali women wear to cover their head and upper body. It's usually worn with a dirac (a long loose-fitting dress). Garbasaaro (plural of garbasaar) come in many beautiful colors and patterns.

Look through the pages of this book and find two popular designs used in Somali shawls.

Mamas use their shawls in so many ways.
When Guled was a baby his mama used to feed
him milk under her shawl, and use it to carry him
on her back.

Sometimes the shawl was a canopy for them to play under. This would make baby Guled giggle and kick!

Now that he is older, mama's shawl is a floppy hand that he holds when they go out. He likes to tug it gently to get her attention and show her things in the market.

The women at the market love to show mama new shawls she can buy.

Guled's favorite colors are yellow and green. Today he picked a yellow shawl for mama to buy.

Sometimes Guled hides under a shawl and pretends he's a monster to scare mama.

At prayer time, Guled wraps himself in mama's shawl. His mama told him that boys don't need shawls to pray, but it makes praying even more fun.

Mama's shawl is a cozy place to sleep in the afternoon. Mama tucks Guled tight until he feels snug like a caterpillar in a cocoon.

When Guled's sister Bilan was born, mama used to give her milk under her shawl too.

When Guled and Bilan play on the floor, they sit on mama's shawl and pretend it's a magic carpet!

Every night, mama reads books to them while they're all wrapped in her shawl together. It feels like they are in a quiet cave.

Mama's shawl always smells so good! That's because she puts uunsi near her clothes after she washes them. The smell reminds Guled of smokey flowers.

Uunsi is a type of perfumed incense used in Somalia.

When Guled goes outside, he sees mamas wearing shawls are all around. They look like superheroes in bright capes!

Books by Idil Ismail

Available through Amazon and all major book sellers. For large orders please email mosaicpublishers@gmail.com

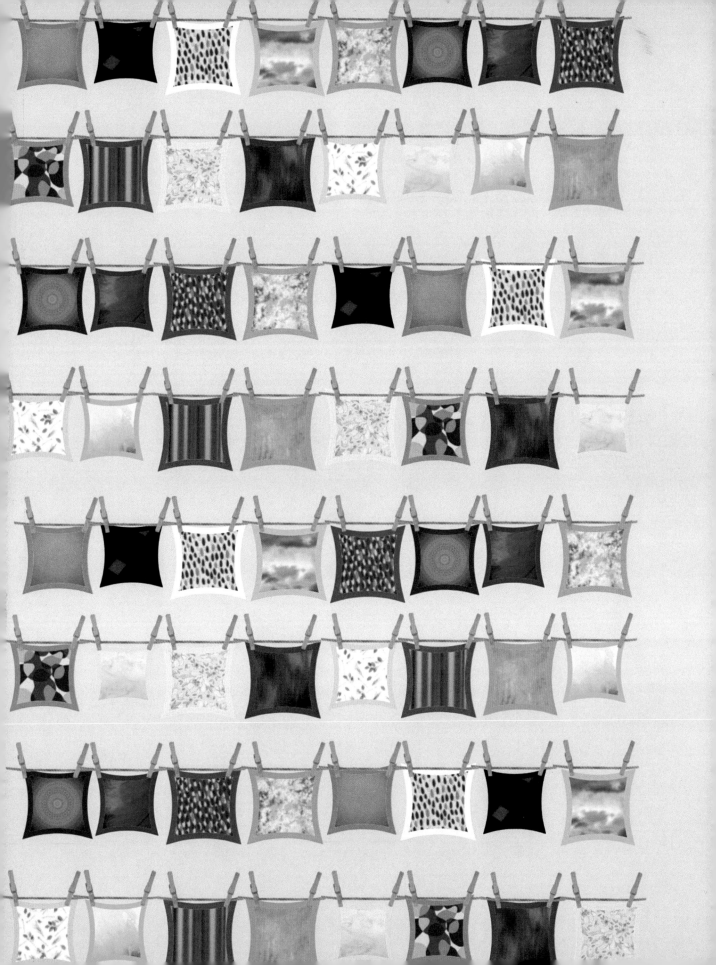

Made in the USA
Middletown, DE
15 March 2023

26754812R10022